Delightful Delilah

Nigel Gray & Anna Pignataro

Lothian
BOOKS

When Dad came home from work on Monday, Ewan was helping Mum cook dinner.

'Hello, Ewan,' said Dad.

'My name's not Ewan,'
said Ewan.
'It's Mark.'
Dad looked at Mum.
She shrugged.
'He's changed his name
to Mark,' she said.
'It's like reMARKable,'
Ewan said.
'You're right,' said Dad,
'it is.'

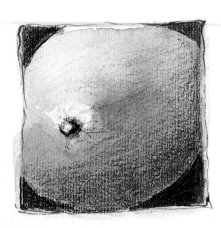

When Dad came home from
work on Tuesday, Ewan
was digging for worms
in the garden.
'Hello, Mark,' Dad said.
'It's not just Mark,' Ewan said.
'It's Mark Orange.'
'Oh,' said Dad. 'You mean Mark
Orange like the colour?'
'No,' said Ewan,
'like the fruit.'
'OK,' said Dad.

When Dad came home
from work on Wednesday,
Ewan was bouncing on
the trampoline with
Cookie Monster, the dog.
'Hi, Mark Orange,' said Dad.
'It's not just Mark Orange,' said Ewan.
'It's Mark Orange Apple.'
'Who are you going to be
tomorrow?' asked Dad.
'Mark Orange Apple Banana?'
'NO,' said Ewan scornfully.
'Banana's not a NAME!'
'What about Mark
Fruit Salad?' said Dad.
'Don't be silly, Dad,' said Ewan.

When Dad came home from work on Thursday, Ewan had lined up six snails on the garden path.

'They're going to have a race,' said Ewan.

'I hope they don't get too puffed out, Ewan,' said Dad.

'My name is *not* Ewan,' said Ewan angrily.

'Oops, sorry!' said Dad. 'What's your name today, my old fruit?'

'I'm *not* a fruit,' said Ewan. 'My name is Ernie and Bert!'

'What, *both* of them?' said Dad.

'Yes,' said Ewan. 'Lots of people have two names.'

When Dad came home from work on Friday, Mum was helping Ewan make a cubby behind the garage. 'Hello, Ernie and Bert,' said Dad.

'I'm not Ernie and Bert,'
said Ewan, 'I'm Delilah.'
'Delilah,' said Dad, looking at Mum.
'But that's a ...'
Mum shook her head. 'We heard it in a
song on the radio,' Mum said. 'He liked it.'
'It's like DELIGHTFUL,' said Ewan.
'You're right,' said Dad. 'It is.'

On Saturday morning Mum went away for the weekend. Ewan and Dad saw her off at the train station.

Back home, Ewan made a
train out of cardboard cartons
and took his teddies for a trip.

After lunch Dad said to Ewan,
'Hop in the car, Delilah.'
'Where are we going?' asked Ewan.
'To   somebody's house.'
'Whose house?'
'A friend of mine from work. His name is
Mark — just like yours used to be.'
'That was <u>ages</u> ago,' said Ewan.

At Mark's house Mark said to Ewan, 'This is my little girl. She's the same age as you.'

'What's your name?' Ewan asked the little girl. 'DELILAH,' said Delilah.

Ewan was struck dumb for a moment.
Then he shouted,
'No, it's not! That's my name.
You can't take my name!'
'It's my name', shouted Delilah,
stamping her foot. 'It can't be
your name. You're a boy!'

The dads had to pull them apart
or there would have been a fight.
'This was a mistake', said Ewan's dad.
'I'm sorry.'

When Mum
came home on
Sunday, Ewan
was helping Dad
iron a shirt.
'Hello,
Delilah,'
Mum said.

'Don't call me that!' shouted Ewan.
'That's not my name!'
'Well, you're certainly not being
delightful,' said Mum. 'So what is your name?'
'Don't you know anything?' said Ewan.
'His name is Ewan,' said Dad.
'Ewan,' said Mum. 'That's my
favourite name. I love that name.'
'So do I,' said Dad.

'You 'n' me, kid,'
he said to Ewan.
'You 'n' me, Dad,'
said Ewan, smiling.
'Ewan me!'

For Scarlett, Campbell and Juliett. NG
For Veronica, Matilda and Oskar. AP

Thomas C. Lothian Pty Ltd
132 Albert Road, South Melbourne, Victoria 3205
www.lothian.com.au

First published 2002

National Library of Australia
Cataloguing-in-Publication data:

Gray, Nigel, 1941- .
  Delightful Delilah / Nigel Gray & Anna Pignataro.

  For children.
  ISBN 0 7344 0377 1 (pbk.).

  1. Names, Personal — Juvenile fiction. I. Pignataro, Anna.
  II. Title.

A823.3

Designed by Sandra Nobes
Prepress by Digital Imaging Group, Port Melbourne
Printed in China by Leefung-Asco